The
Bottlenose Dolphin

The Bottlenose Dolphin

By Virginia Schomp

DILLON PRESS
New York

Acknowledgments

The author is most grateful to Dana Carnegie of the Dolphin Research Center for her expert assistance.

Photo Credits

Photo research by Debbie Needleman

Cover courtesy of Marineland of Florida

Back cover courtesy of Sea World of Florida

Eric Martin: frontispiece, 20; Sea World of Florida: title page, 8, 14, 17; Laurel Canty/Dolphin Research Center: 12, 24-25, 30, 31, 39, 52; Marty Snyderman: 27; Pieter Folkens/Earth Views: 33; John Domant/Center for Marine Conservation: 40; Scott Sinclair/Earth Views: 34; Marineland of Florida; 42, 45, 47, 48, 49, 51

Book design by Carol Matsuyama

Library of Congress Cataloging-in-Publication Data

Schomp, Virginia (Virginia Anne)
    The bottlenose dolphin / by Virginia Schomp. — 1st ed.
      p. cm. — (Remarkable animals)
    Includes index.
    ISBN 0-87518-605-X   0-382-24724-8 (pbk.)
    1. Atlantic bottlenosed dolphin—Juvenile literature. 2. Endangered species—Juvenile literature. [1. Bottlenosed dolphins. 2. Dolphins.] I. Title. II. Series: Dillon remarkable animals book.
    QL737.C432S425   1994
    599.5'3—dc20   93-37927

Summary: Describes the physical characteristics, ancestry, habitat, and life cycle of the bottlenose dolphin, with an explanation of the threat humans pose to its survival.

Dillon Press   Maxwell Macmillan Canada, Inc.
Macmillan Publishing Company   1200 Eglinton Avenue East
866 Third Avenue   Suite 200
New York, NY 10022   Don Mills, Ontario M3C 3N1

Macmillan Publishing Company is part of the Maxwell Communication Group of Companies.

First edition

Printed in the United States of America

10 9 8 7 6 5 4 3

Contents

Facts about the Bottlenose Dolphin

Scientific Name: *Tursiops truncatus*

Description:

Length—Most are from 8 to 9 feet (2.4 to 2.7 meters) long; individuals have been found measuring 13 feet (4 meters)

Weight—Most are from 400 to 600 pounds (181 to 272 kilograms); individuals have been found weighing up to 1,430 pounds (649 kilograms)

Color—Backs usually are silvery gray; bellies light gray, pink, or white; some all-white (albino) animals have been found

Swimming Speed—Up to 17 mph (27 kph)

Physical Features—Smooth, streamlined body; blowhole on top of head; short beak (also called snout or rostrum) with curved mouth resembling a smile; about 90 sharp teeth, which wear down with age; two flippers; half-moon-shaped dorsal fin on back; strong, tapered tail ending in two horizontal tail flukes

Distinctive Habits: Communicates with clicks, whistles, squeaks, and other sounds; uses echolocation (sound) to find, identify, and pursue objects under water; lives in large schools, or pods, broken down into family groups based on age and sex; gentle and friendly with humans

Food: Many types of fish, shellfish, and mollusks such as squid and octopus; usually swallows fish whole or bites them in half

6

Reproductive Cycle: Female matures at 5 to 12 years, male at age 6 or older; gestation period is 11 to 13 months; female is capable of giving birth every 3 years; newborn calves are strong and well developed, weighing 30 to 40 pounds (14 to 18 kilograms); female raises calf without help of male; calf nurses 2 to 4 years or longer

Life Span: 30 to 40 years

Range: All the world's oceans, except the coldest polar regions

Habitat: Sea waters, including bays, lagoons, and rivers that run into the sea

Chapter 1

Friends from the Sea

Picture yourself on a hot summer day, resting lazily on board a small boat off the coast of Florida. The sun beats down on the clear blue sea, and the gentle waves sparkle like diamonds. Suddenly the calm water bursts to life. A dozen smooth, silvery creatures leap into the air, twist, and fall with a mighty splash. Again and again the remarkable acrobats explode through the surface, showering your small boat with spray. Their power and grace are awesome, and the joy they seem to take in their game makes you laugh with delight. Then, suddenly, as if at some secret signal, the creatures are gone and the sea falls silent again.

Dolphin Myths and Mysteries

The playful, graceful sea animals called dolphins have fascinated people for centuries. Engravings of dolphins have been discovered on the walls of prehistoric caves in South Africa. Ancient Greek and Roman legends tell of dolphins befriending people, especially children, and even carrying drowning swimmers to safety. Fishermen have long considered dolphins a sign of fair weather and good luck, and in their traditional stories dolphins are their helpers, herding fish into their nets.

In modern times many people regarded these ancient tales as fables or myths, not the truth. But studies of dolphins over the past few decades have begun to change that point of view. Today scientists believe that many of these wonderful stories were based on fact. Through their continuing observations of dolphins in the wild and in marine parks and aquariums, we are just beginning to unravel some of the mysteries surrounding this ancient friend from the sea.

An Extraordinary Bond

At the Dolphin Research Center in Florida, a dolphin named Aleta waits patiently while a little boy gropes for a hold on its **dorsal fin***, then circles the pool with the delighted child in tow. The boy has Down's syndrome, a condition that limits his physical and mental development. Aleta is one of the dolphins chosen to help with his treatment. "The animals are gentle with him, as if they understand he's different," says the boy's doctor. "There's a rapport [closeness] between them I can't explain."

Many stories illustrate this extraordinary rapport between humans and dolphins. In 1955 a young female dolphin began to swim among the bathers at Opononi Beach in New Zealand. Named Opo by the local townspeople, the dolphin visited each day to play with the children. It would toss a beach ball or empty bottles and leap triumphantly into the air at the crowd's applause. Opo chose one young girl as a special friend. Whenever that girl went into the water, the dolphin would leave the other children to

---

* Words in **bold type** are explained in the glossary at the end
  of this book.

At Florida's Dolphin Research Center, a bottlenose dolphin makes therapy fun for a child with Down's syndrome.

dive between her legs and lift her for a ride.

Further evidence of a special bond can be found in the age-old stories of dolphins and people "fishing" together. According to ancient legends, a small tribe of fishermen called the Imragen, who live on the coast of Mauritania, in northwest Africa, count on the dolphins for help in their work. Scientists doubted these stories until the early 1970s, when a team of researchers visited Mauritania. There they witnessed a remarkable scene. As a fisherman stood on shore beating the water with sticks, the sea began to churn. A large group of dolphins appeared, herding a school of fish toward land and into the waiting fishermen's nets.

The Imragen and other people who depend on **cooperative fishing** with dolphins believe that their friends from the sea help them intentionally. Most scientists disagree. They think that dolphins work with fishermen to satisfy their own needs—when the fish are trapped, both humans and dolphins get their share of the feast.

Dolphins cooperate with one another, too, in the hunt for food. A group of dolphins hunting together may surround a school of fish. Then they take turns feeding, a few dolphins at a time, while the others keep the fish trapped inside the circle.

"Baby-sitters" and "Lifeguards"

Hunting together is not the only way dolphins cooperate. When a dolphin calf is born, female dolphins gather around to protect the infant from sharks or overly curious male dolphins. Later the females may help the mother by "baby-sitting." While the mother feeds, a group of dolphins forms a moving "playpen," with the calf swimming safely inside.

Dolphins also help one another in times of trouble. A group of dolphins often will **stand by,** or refuse to leave, a wounded or sick member. If one of the group is caught in fishing nets, others may try, without success, to help by biting at the lines or charging the fishing boat. A badly injured dolphin may get special help. By placing their heads under the wounded animal's flippers, two dolphins can keep another afloat until it is able to swim on its own again.

There have been reports of dolphins rescuing people in much the same way. For example, a woman who nearly drowned while swimming off a deserted beach in Florida was pushed to shore by a dolphin.

There has always been a remarkable bond between dolphins and humans--especially children.

Most scientists doubt that this kind of rescue is intentional. Instead they think that these dolphin "lifeguards" are simply following the same instinct, or natural impulse, that makes them help another dolphin in trouble. Of course, to a drowning swimmer saved by a helpful dolphin, it's the action, not the intention, that counts!

"Seeing" with the Ears

How does a dolphin let the members of its group know it's in trouble? It calls for help! Dolphins have a large "vocabulary" of sounds. They whistle, click, grunt, squeak, squawk, and wail. These sounds make up the simple "language" dolphins use to communicate.

Before it is a year old, a dolphin can whistle its own "name." That unique sound, called its **signature whistle,** tells other dolphins who it is. Dolphins also can imitate one another's signature whistles. Two dolphins separated in dark waters might never find each other by sight alone. So they call to each other,

A group of bottlenose dolphins glides gracefully through the water.

combining signature whistles as if to say, "Mother, this is Opo." More sounds can be added for more information: "Mother, this is Opo, in trouble."

Dolphins also make sounds that are too high-pitched for humans to hear. These quick, high clicks are part of the animal's **echolocation** system. Just as bats use sound to "see" in the dark, dolphins use echolocation to find and identify objects in the often murky ocean waters. By interpreting the *echo*es of its own signals bouncing off objects, a dolphin can *locate* a tasty fish or swim safely around an underwater reef.

Learning about Dolphins

Most studies of the sounds dolphins make have been done with the bottlenose dolphin. This type of dolphin adapts quickly to aquarium life and is remarkably gentle and friendly with humans.

Bottlenose dolphins also learn quickly, and they often amaze observers with their gift for imitating sound and movement. Sometimes they copy the behavior of penguins, turtles, or other animals— including people. In one marine park a trainer blew a puff of smoke against the window of a tank where a six-month-old bottlenose dolphin was watching. The calf raced to its mother and returned to the glass to spit out a "puff" of milk.

Contacts like these with bottlenose dolphins have

provided clues to their behavior and their unusual intelligence. But watching dolphins in artificial environments brings us only one small step closer to understanding this remarkable animal. In the past few years researchers have begun observing dolphins in their natural surroundings. The challenges these people face are as vast as the ocean itself. Dolphins and humans live in two separate worlds. An ancient bond reaches across that gulf. But much of the life of a dolphin living free in the sea remains a mystery.

The bottlenose dolphin takes its name from its blunt, rounded beak.

Chapter 2

Suited for Swimming

"They exchanged the land for the sea and put on the form of fishes."

That's how an ancient Greek writer described the dolphin—a creature that is as much at home in the water as any fish but is not a fish at all. Dolphins are **mammals.** Unlike fish, they are warm-blooded, which means that they create their own body heat and that their temperature stays even instead of going up and down with their environment. And like other mammals, including humans, dolphins breathe air, give birth to their young live (rather than laying eggs), and nurse their newborns with milk.

All whales, porpoises, and dolphins belong to the same **order,** or major group, of mammals. In that order, called Cetacea, there are about 80 **species,** groups of animals that have many similar characteristics. The bottlenose dolphin species gets its scientific name from its familiar blunt beak. *Tursiops truncatus* comes from two Latin words: *tursiops* for "a fish resembling a dolphin" and *truncatus* for "cut off." The bottlenose dolphin's cut-off beak is drawn back in a natural curve—the built-in "smile" that to humans is one of this friendly animal's most charming features.

Whales, Porpoises, and Dolphins

What do you think of when you hear the word *whale*? Chances are you picture a fish as big as a mountain. Whales can be huge. In fact, the orca, or killer whale, is one of the largest **predators** on earth, growing as long as 31 feet (9.4 meters) and weighing up to 18,000 pounds (8,163 kilograms). At the opposite end of the scale is the melon-headed whale, named for its rounded profile. The melon-head grows to just under 9 feet (2.7 meters).

As different as these two creatures may seem,

they still have a lot in common. So scientists lump them together, along with about 30 similar members of the cetacean order, in a smaller grouping called a **family.** That family, Delphinidea, or dolphins, includes animals that may be named whales (like the killer whale) or dolphins (like the bottlenose dolphin). But to the scientist, they're all still dolphins.

To make things more difficult, many people confuse dolphins with porpoises. According to most scientists, dolphins and porpoises are similar, but they are not the same animal and they do not belong to the same family. In fact, only six species of small, sturdy, beakless cetaceans should really be called porpoises.

The true members of the dolphin family include many intriguing species. The hourglass dolphin has dramatic black and white markings in an hourglass design. The Atlantic spotted dolphin can swim as fast as 25 mph (40 kph). The spinner dolphin is famous for its high, spinning leaps. But to humans,

The natural curve of their beaks lets these friendly dolphins "smile" for the camera.

the best-known and most beloved of them all is the bottlenose dolphin.

"The Form of Fishes"

A foot below the ocean's surface a group of bottlenose dolphins lies nearly motionless. Then, slowly, a great silvery shadow rises to the surface, lets out a soft sound like a puff of wind, and sinks again. One by one, every few minutes, the other dolphins follow. What are they doing?

They're sleeping! Or, more exactly, dozing in a state as close to sleep as an adult dolphin ever comes. For the dolphin is an animal that lives in the water but breathes the air. Every few minutes it must surface to breathe. If it doesn't, it will drown.

Breathe in and then out. You've just traded about 15 percent of the stale air in your lungs for fresh air. Each time the bottlenose dolphin breathes, it exchanges 80 to 90 percent of the air in its lungs. That allows dolphins to breathe less often than humans do. In fact, active bottlenose dolphins breathe only

The orca is the largest and most powerful member of the dolphin family.

once or twice a minute. During a deep dive, they can go as long as seven minutes between breaths.

A dolphin breathes through its **blowhole,** a kind of nostril on the top of its head. If you've ever been snorkeling, you know how much easier it is to swim when you don't have to lift your face out of the water to breathe. The bottlenose dolphin can glide swiftly through the water, breathing with only its blowhole exposed.

The blowhole is just one of the ways this remarkable animal has **adapted** to life in the water. For millions of years ago, as the ancient Greek writer tells us, the dolphins left the land and "put on the form of fishes."

From Land to Sea

By studying **fossils** and bones, scientists have learned much about the **evolution** of dolphins. They believe that in prehistoric times the ancestors of the dolphins had hair, four legs, and a long tail. For some reason, about 50 million years ago, these creatures began to look to the sea for food. The animals with features that helped them live in the water had the best chance of surviving and reproducing. Over time a very different-looking animal evolved—one remarkably well suited to its new environment.

The dolphins lost their hair—it had slowed down their swimming and wasn't much good at keeping them warm underwater. In its place they developed a layer of blubber. This thin jacket of fat holds in their body heat and helps them to float.

The blubber makes up the third layer of the dolphin's soft, elastic skin. The top layer of skin is shed every couple of hours, keeping the dolphin's skin remarkably smooth so it can glide swiftly through the water.

Adding to the dolphin's speed is its **streamlined** shape. The hind legs have long since disappeared. The front legs have evolved into a pair of flippers, used for steering and balance. Also used for balance is the dorsal fin—the high, curved triangle on the dolphin's back that sometimes leads panicky

The bottlenose dolphin breathes through a blowhole on top of its head.

swimmers to mistake this gentle creature for a shark.

Where its ancestors had a long and probably pointed tail, the dolphin now has a gracefully curved tail ending in a powerful paddle. That paddle consists of two tail flukes—flat, horizontal (running from side to side) lobes with a notch in between.

Watch a fish in a tank and you'll notice that its tail is vertical and that it swims by moving this upright tail from side to side. But the dolphin moves its powerful tail flukes up and down. That lets it rise and dive quickly, a real advantage when chasing a meal or trying not to become one.

Dolphins often use their powerful tails to leap from the water in a series of curves as they swim.

Dolphins use their flippers for steering and balance.

This is called "porpoising" or "running." Porpoising bottlenose dolphins can reach speeds of up to 17 mph (27 kph). They can go even faster by "bow riding." Many sailors and other seagoers have been delighted by the sight of a group of dolphins taking turns riding on the wave created by the bow, or forward part, of a fast-moving ship. Bottlenose dolphins also have been seen "body surfing" on waves breaking near shore. There is no scientific explanation for this behavior: The dolphins just seem to enjoy the ride!

A Super Sense
The bottlenose dolphin has no sense of smell—have you ever tried to smell something underwater? It

does have taste buds, but scientists aren't certain what role taste plays in its life. The sense of touch is a big part of the dolphin's social life. The animals often swim with their sides brushing, rub against one another, and caress with their beaks and flippers.

The dolphin's eyesight usually is well developed, too. Captive bottlenose dolphins have leaped from the water to catch a fish held as high as 20 feet (6 meters) above their tank. **Monocular vision** gives them another advantage—a mother dolphin can search for food or predators with her right eye while her left looks after a wandering calf.

But good eyesight isn't much use in cloudy water, and even in the clearest water, sound travels faster and farther than light. So for an animal that lives in the water, hearing is more important than sight. And the bottlenose dolphin has such superior hearing that even a blind dolphin can survive well in the wild.

The bottlenose dolphin can hear sounds that are nearly eight times beyond the human upper limit.

A pair of porpoising dolphins make their own waves.

Only bats have keener hearing. Using that well-developed hearing and its echolocation ability, the dolphin can chase a swift fish, find its way about the sea, or catch the far-off cry of a fellow dolphin in trouble.

Super hearing is just one more way the dolphin has adapted to the demands of its environment. With its keen senses, ultrasmooth skin, streamlined body, and powerful tail, the dolphin is in perfect harmony with its watery home.

Nearly all the world's oceans are home to the bottlenose dolphin.

Chapter 3

Life in the Sea

Off the coast of South Africa a group of bottlenose dolphins takes up the chase. Two swift lines meeting in a spearhead, they race toward a sheltered bay. Suddenly they reassemble in one long line and leap toward land, driving a school of fish before them. A few dolphins speed on ahead, then turn back toward the main line. The fish are trapped in between. The line dissolves, and the dolphins rush into the school, seizing fish after fish and swallowing them whole.

Like the dolphins that "fish" with the Imragen tribe, these bottlenose dolphins are using one of their many very effective methods of cooperative fishing. Dolphins nearly always hunt together. Alone, a dolphin can chase only one fish at a time. Together, a group can surround an entire school like a living net, or herd their prey toward the surface or toward shallow water, and eat their fill. Groups of bottlenose dolphins have even been seen chasing fish across breaking waves onto shore, wriggling out of the water to claim their meal, then riding out on the next wave.

A meal to a dolphin can be just about anything that swims. Bottlenose dolphins eat a wide variety of fish, including mullet, catfish, anchovies, and sardines, plus squid, eels, octopus, shrimp, and crabs. Those meals serve a double purpose—surrounded by water it cannot drink, the dolphin gets the fresh water it needs from the body of the fish it eats.

A Home without Walls

The earth is 71 percent ocean. And the bottlenose dolphin lives in practically all the world's oceans, except the coldest polar waters.

Scientists believe there are two types of bottle-nose dolphins—one that lives within a few miles of land (coastal dolphins) and one that lives farther out to sea (offshore dolphins). Coastal dolphins sometimes venture inland, into bays, lagoons, and shallow rivers that run into the ocean. And even offshore dolphins rarely travel farther than about 500 miles (800 kilometers) out to sea.

Dolphins have no real "home," no cozy den or burrow or nest all their own. But within their vast watery **habitat,** they do have a **home range.** In that strictly defined area the dolphin hunts, plays, sleeps, mates, and raises its young.

The size of the bottlenose dolphin's home range varies in different parts of the world. It can stretch more than 250 miles (402 kilometers) along the coast of South Africa or less than 10 miles (16 kilometers) along Florida's shores.

The Bountiful Sea

In all the world the bottlenose dolphin has only three

natural predators: false killer whales, pilot whales, and sharks. Those enemies usually prey on young, injured, or sick dolphins. Sometimes, though, they will attack a healthy adult, and older dolphins often carry shark-bite scars. Yet there also have been cases of captive dolphins living peacefully in the same tank with a shark. Perhaps when food is easy to come by, the shark no longer finds the dolphin a tempting meal.

The bottlenose dolphin has strong defenses against its few enemies. Full-grown bottlenose dolphins are large and powerful. They average from 8 to 9 feet (2.4 to 2.7 meters) long and may weigh from 400 to 600 pounds (181 to 272 kilograms). They are fast, hardy swimmers, with sharp teeth, a strong beak, and a powerful tail. And they have another defense—their natural coloring.

The back and sides of most bottlenose dolphins are silvery gray, although they can be purplish gray, black, or brown. The belly is light gray, pink, or white. Whatever its exact color, the dolphin is always

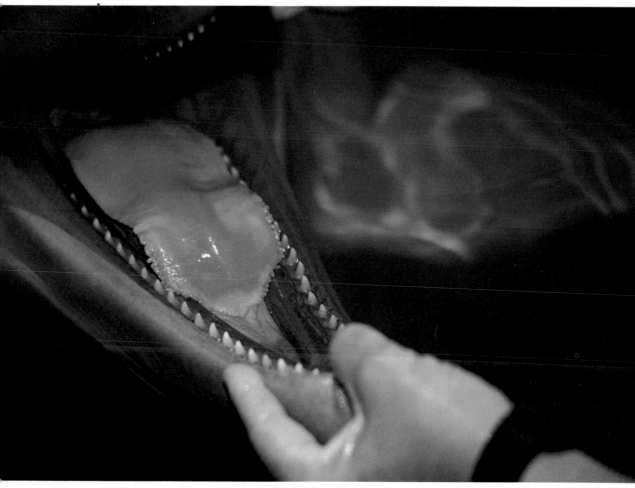
The bottlenose dolphin has about 90 large, sharp teeth.

darker above and lighter below. That shading acts as **camouflage.** From above, the dolphin's back seems to melt into the dark waters; from below, its pale belly blends with the light.

40

With the help of its natural coloring, the bottle-nose dolphin has thrived in its wide, watery home. To the dolphin, the sea has served for centuries as shelter, food pantry, and watering hole all in one.

Dark on top and pale below, this dolphin's natural coloring blends with its environment.

This female bottlenose dolphin is about to become a mother.

Chapter 4

The Dolphin Family

In the blue light beneath the ocean's surface, a group of female bottlenose dolphins forms a circle. A heavy gray female is in the center. She is behaving oddly, bending her tail down and up, down and up, almost as if she were exercising. After half an hour a small, soft, folded dolphin tail emerges. Two hours later an infant dolphin falls free.

Eyes wide open, the calf rises to the surface for its first breath. It looks like a miniature version of its mother. About 3 feet (1 meter) long—one-third its mother's length—and weighing about 30 to 40 pounds (14 to 18 kilograms), it has a limp dorsal fin and soft, curled tail flukes. Its head is a little too big for its body, and on its beak are a few whiskers, reminders of its land-based ancestors. It is covered in creases where its skin was folded inside its mother's body.

Like the calf of a cow, the newborn dolphin is strong and well developed. It can keep its body warm, swim without help, and observe the world. But it is still an infant. Its swimming is wobbly, and it shoots its whole head out of the water to breathe. This baby will need plenty of parenting before it is ready to survive on its own.

Dolphin Motherhood

After the dolphin calf takes its first breath, its mother prods it into a spot just beside her dorsal fin. Here it will remain for most of the next few months. The calf's dorsal fin will stand up, and its tail flukes will harden. It will lose its creases and whiskers. The teeth that were just below its gums at birth will break through. The calf may try out those teeth on a scrap of fish soon. But for now, its whole diet is its mother's milk.

It is fortunate that mother dolphins have just

The calf's small, folded tail emerges.

one calf at a time, because raising a baby dolphin is a full-time job. Young dolphins are curious and playful, and that can make them wander. A calf alone is an easy target for predators. Mother dolphins whistle for their wandering offspring, listening for the calf's faint, quavery return call. Sometimes the calf tries to turn its mother's pursuit into a game. Then the mother may give it a warning by slapping the water with her tail or shoving the calf with her beak. She might even press the mischievous young-ster to the surface or the bottom of the water for a little "time-out."

At about three months the calf begins to experience a little more freedom. But as long as the youngster is nursing, the dolphin mother never com-pletely relaxes her guard. And although bottlenose dolphins usually try their first solid food at about six months, they continue nursing for another year and a half, and sometimes for as long as four years. Often a calf will nurse until its mother gives birth again. A mature female dolphin can have a calf about every three years throughout her life, and she may live to be 30 or 40. That's a lot of mothering!

A Place in the Family

The dolphin calf grows quickly. At two months it weighs twice its birth weight, and by age one its length has increased by 2 feet (0.6 meters). It will soon be time to find a new place in the dolphin family.

Dolphins are social animals. They rarely live alone. Bottlenose dolphins usually live in large schools, or **pods,** broken down into separate family groups. Groups of coastal bottlenose dolphins average about 10 members, while offshore groups may number 100 or more. But group size can change from season to season or even from day to day. An animal that appears in one group today may join another tomorrow—or just pop in for a visit.

It is difficult to observe the behavior of dolphins roaming free in the sea. Some studies have been

The emerging infant's tail flukes are curled and soft.

made of large schools in specific areas. These have shown that bottlenose dolphin groups probably are based on age and sex. One group may include mothers with calves, while another may be made up of adult males. Young "bachelor" males and females may live in separate groups or in a combined group of preadult males and females.

A youngster living in a group of mothers with calves is well cared for. There are many eyes to look after it and many ears, too. The members of the group are able to combine their echolocation skills, making them even more efficient at spotting predators as well as **prey.**

Group living also is a good way for young dolphins to find out about the world. Calves discover the

Slowly, a new bottlenose dolphin makes its way into the world.

limits of their home range. They learn how to identify one another, how to find and capture prey, and how to recognize and avoid predators. And they learn the role each member of the group plays in dolphin society.

Young female dolphins sometimes stay with their mothers all their lives, while young males usually leave to join the bachelors at age six or older. But even the most adventurous youngster never completely forgets its mother. When it is frightened or hurt, it may return to swim by her side. Young dolphins may drop by to see a new baby brother or sister. And a young female who has tried independence may re-join her mother's group when she becomes a mother herself.

A New Life

It is early spring, and off the coast of North Carolina a school of dolphins passes swiftly and silently northward. On the edges of their dorsal fins and flukes ride clusters of firmly attached barnacles. To the area's fishermen, those small, hard-shelled hitchhikers identify the school as the "tassel-fins"— bottlenose dolphins that pass by each spring and autumn on their annual **migration.**

Not all bottlenose dolphins migrate. Some schools stay in the same home range year-round. But in regions where seasonal changes mean changes in the food supply, dolphins must go where the fishing is good.

In many areas spring or early summer is the

time when bottlenose dolphins return to their home range. Often this also is the season for dolphin births. But as the bottlenose dolphin lives in so many different parts of the world, it is not surprising that the birth season varies. In fact, depending on an area's climate, bottlenose dolphin calves may be born at nearly any time of the year.

Female bottlenose dolphins are ready to begin reproducing at anywhere from age 5 to 12, males at about age 6 or older. The adult male bottlenose dolphin is very determined when seeking out a female. For several days he follows her, showing his interest by prodding with his beak and loudly clicking, or "popping," his jaws. When at last the female responds, the pair mates, and then the male goes his separate way. Although female bottlenose dolphins are devoted mothers, there does not seem to be any special bond between male dolphins and their offspring.

The pregnant female dolphin stays close to the rest of the group while she carries her calf. Finally,

The newborn calf looks like a junior version of its mother.

after 11 to 13 months, the time for the infant's birth draws near. The many days it has spent inside its mother's body lets the calf emerge strong and sturdy. Another bottlenose dolphin is ready to learn about life in the great sea, secure within the shelter of the dolphin family.

Chapter 5

Dolphins Endangered

The greatest threat to dolphins is not hungry whales or sharks. It is people.

People threaten dolphins by damaging their natural environment. Overfishing wipes out the small fish the dolphins need for survival. Pollution of the seas kills both fish and marine (sea) mammals. Between 1987 and 1988 over half of all the bottle-nose dolphins living off the Atlantic coast of the United States fell victim to pollution. To one observer, the dead and injured dolphins looked "as though they had been dipped in acid."

Dolphins also are killed accidentally by large-scale fisheries. Large schools of tuna often swim beneath dolphins. When nets are lowered to catch

Ocean pollution endangers dolphins and other sea mammals.

the tuna, dolphins are frequently caught, too. They are trapped underwater in the strong nets and drown, or they are injured or killed when they are thrown overboard as the nets are emptied. In the past three decades about six million dolphins have died in tuna nets. Many others have been killed in nets set for shrimp, sharks, and other fish.

Because of all these threats, the survival of some species of dolphins is in danger. Nearly 80 percent of the world's spinner dolphins have been destroyed. Other species are threatened, too.

Hope for the Future

Laws have been passed to protect the dolphins. The U.S. Marine Mammal Protection Act of 1972 made it illegal to kill or capture marine mammals in U.S. waters or to import them into the United States, except for dolphins taken under a special permit for aquariums or for scientific experiments. The law also set a limit on the number of dolphins that could be killed accidentally by tuna fisheries. In 1989 the

United Nations General Assembly passed a resolution limiting the use of drift nets—nets up to 50 miles long that are set adrift in the water to capture whatever swims through them.

But even more must be done. To preserve the supply of fish and spare the lives of dolphins, we must develop and use better fishing methods. To protect the ocean and the animals that live there, more antipollution laws and stronger policing of existing laws are needed.

It will take time and effort for people to undo the damage that's been done. But it will be well worth the cost. From ancient times there has been a special bond between humans and dolphins. This intelligent, playful, gentle animal has given us help and delight. In return we can make certain that the seas never cease to echo with the voice of the remarkable bottlenose dolphin.

Sources of Information about the Bottlenose Dolphin

Ask your librarian to help you find books on whales, porpoises, and dolphins. Some good books include:

Dolphin Days: My Life and Times with the Spinners, Kenneth S. Norris. W. W. Norton, New York, 1991.

Dolphins and Porpoises. Facts on File, New York, 1990.

The Sea World Book of Dolphins, Randall R. Reeves and Stephen Leatherwood. New York, Harcourt Brace Jovanovich, 1987.

You can also get information on the bottlenose dolphin by contacting:

Dolphin Research Center
P.O. Box 522875
Marathon Shores, FL 33052

Glossary

adapted—having changed to fit certain conditions, such as climate, of an animal's or plant's environment

blowhole—nostril in the top of the head of a dolphin

camouflage (KA-muh-flahj)—an animal's coloring (or other characteristic) that acts as a disguise to conceal it from predators

cooperative fishing—dolphins and humans, or a group of dolphins, working together to catch fish

dorsal fin—the high, rubbery appendage, or body part, on the dolphin's back, used for balance; it is shaped like a half-moon, curving toward the tail

echolocation—a way of finding objects by bouncing sound waves off them

evolution—the changes an animal or plant undergoes over time

family—a scientific grouping of plants or animals, smaller than *order* and larger than *species;* the bottlenose dolphin belongs to the family Delphinidea

fossils—the hardened remains or traces of a plant or animal that lived long ago

habitat (HAB-ih-tat)—the type of area (such as grasslands, desert, or the sea) in which a plant or animal normally lives

home range—the geographical area to which an animal normally limits its activities

mammals—animals that are warm-blooded, breathe air, give birth to their young live, and nurse their young with milk

migration—moving from one area to another for feeding or breeding

monocular (mah-NAH-kyuh-ler) vision—the ability to see with each eye independently at the same time

order—a broad scientific grouping of animals and plants based on their shared characteristics; orders are broken down into smaller, more closely related groups: *family, genus,* and *species.* The bottlenose dolphin belongs to the order Cetacea.

pod—a number of dolphins living together; also called a school

predator (PREHD-uh-ter)—an animal that hunts other animals for food

prey—an animal hunted for food by another animal

signature whistle—the one-of-a-kind sound a bottlenose dolphin makes to identify itself to other dolphins

species (SPEE-sheez)—a group of animals or plants having many similar characteristics

standing by—one of the ways dolphins help one another; when a dolphin is injured or sick, its group may stay nearby for hours, ready to help or protect it

streamlined—shaped with smooth, flowing lines for greater speed

Index

"My best childhood memories are of summer vacations in Florida," says Virginia Schomp, "when we watched the dolphins play from a rocky pier off the Gulf Coast. Today we live in a pine woods by a broad lake, but sometimes, when a storm whips the water the right shade of gray, I can almost see the graceful curve of a dolphin riding the waves."

A freelance editor and writer, Ms. Schomp is the author of two books for the Better Business Bureau. This is her first book for young readers. She lives in Monticello, in New York's Catskill Mountains, with her husband, their son, Chip, and his dog, Dale.